Laude

Laude

*For Simone and for Karen*

Text copyright © 1987 M.L. Miller,
illustration © 1987 Verlag Neugebauer Press, Salzburg, Austria.
Published in North America by Picture Book Studio Ltd.,
Distributed in USA by Picture Book Studio Ltd., Natick, MA.
Distributed in Canada by Vanwell Publishing, St. Catharines.
Published in UK by Picture Book Studio, Neugebauer Press Ltd., London.
Distributed in UK by Ragged Bears, Andover.
Distributed in Australia by Era Publications, Adelaide.
All rights reserved.
Printed in Italy by Grafiche Az, Verona.

LIBRARY OF CONGRESS CATALOGING IN PUBLICATION DATA

Miller, M.L.
Elm tree brown.

Summary: A magical forest aids an escaped robber until he seems too selfish to
help, but after much suffering he proves himself worthy of the forest's protection by
saving a group of orphans from a terrible fate.
[1. Forests and forestry – Fiction. 2. Robbers and outlaws – Fiction. 3. Orphans –
Fiction] I. Friedrich, Daniele, ill. II. Title.
PZ7.M627E1    1987    [Fic]    86-25452
ISBN 0-88708-040-5

Ask your bookseller for this other PICTURE BOOK STUDIO book
by M.L. Miller: DIZZY FROM FOOLS illustrated by Eve Tharlet

M. L. Miller

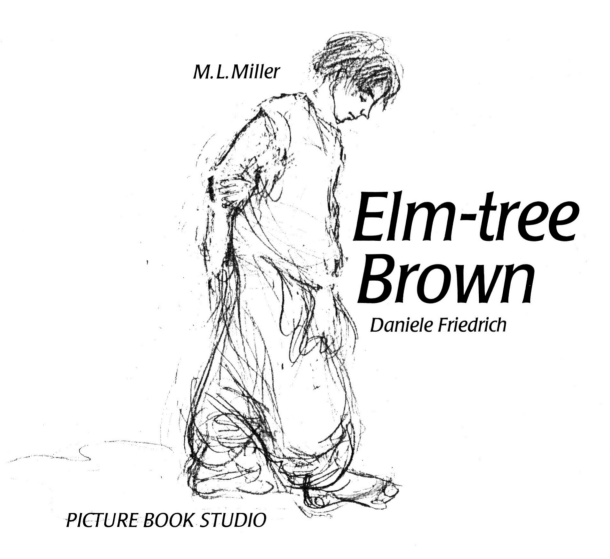

# Elm-tree
# Brown

Daniele Friedrich

PICTURE BOOK STUDIO

A young robber named Theo was thrown into prison for stealing cherry tarts from the Duke's own kitchen – while cleverly disguised as a pot-scrubber. And because he was so clever, he was made to wear a uniform different from all other prisoners – and in the most unpopular shade in the land, elm-tree brown. The other prisoners would have nothing to do with him and whispered about him in sinister voices: "Elm-tree brown, elm-tree brown!"

It was a very cruel prison. The cells were kept freezing cold and the jailers kept most of the food for themselves and kicked any complainers. Theo had to sleep on the floor, with only rags for a cover.

Before long, he was so cold and starving that he knew he must escape soon or be too weak to try. And since he had always been an orphan and had no family to help him, he knew he had to do it all on his own.

So, on Christmas Eve, when the jailers were all sleeping, Theo picked the lock on his cell door with a leftover he had saved when they last had bone soup.

He slipped down a hallway, out through a loose skylight, over the rooftops as a light snow was falling, and down a drainpipe outside the room where the jailers were dreaming.

But no sooner was he over the prison wall than the escape bell sounded. And the Duke's own dragoons, returning from a party, saw his footprints in the snow. "After him!" they yelled from their sleighs. "We'll make short work of *this* jailbird," they chuckled.

Staying in the shadows, Theo ran past a bleak building that he recognized as an orphanage, down a dangerous path, and through a tunnel in a hillside. Just when he felt almost too weak to continue, he came to a gallows by the crossroads. Alarmed, he forced himself to go on – past a factory that snarled and buzzed in the night – until he found himself in a flat, open field.

Then, as the moon broke through the clouds, the dragoons rode into view. "The jailbird!" they barked. And, seeing his uniform for the first time, they hissed with disgust, "An elm-tree brown, elm-tree brown!" and they doubled their efforts to catch him.

All hope seemed lost to Theo. When suddenly he saw, rising up ahead as though from a dream, a dense forest. With his last ounce of strength he staggered in among the trees, with the dragoons close behind.

The dragoons screeched to a halt. For there in the moonlight, with not a snowflake upon it, was a forest of elm trees, each one elm-tree brown!

Gritting their teeth, the dragoons charged into the woods. The robber was close by. But he blended so well with the trees that he was almost invisible. And the dragoons finally gave up and went home, feeling cheated of a good capture.

When they were gone, Theo, weary and starving, stood in the woods and looked around and said, "O Forest, O Forest, thank you for saving my life on this cold, lonely night. Can I ever repay you?"

But the forest made not a murmur.

Then, fearing the dragoons would return, he went deeper into the forest. And he discovered it was not one forest at all, but four forests growing together, and each in a different season. Behind the wintry elm trees was a forest of peach trees in the full bloom of spring. Then came a forest of willows in the warm greens of summer. There he thawed out and ate from some berry bushes. Then came a forest of purple-black plum trees in the brisk chill of autumn.

Theo was so amazed that he ran from forest to forest, laughing wildly at his great change of luck, until he fell down exhausted in the willows of summer. And as he was falling asleep, an idea took hold of his mind. He knew it was wrong, but he could not resist it. He would get even with the evil Duke for throwing him into that cruel prison. Like Robin Hood, he would steal from the rich and give to the poor, and he would *never* be captured again.

So, on New Year's Eve, while the nobles celebrated at the Duke's castle, Theo slipped from the forest of peach trees and kept to the back roads. He did not look like a robber, but like a man going to a costume party. For he wore an outfit made entirely of peach blossoms, sewn with thread from his prison suit and a twig for a needle.

At midnight, as the nobles greeted the New Year with noise-makers and fancy cakes, Theo was in the treasury counting diamonds into a sack. But he was discovered, and could only escape by swinging across the ballroom on a chandelier and leaping out into the night.

"After him, dragoons!" ordered the Duke. "A bandit in peach blossoms can't be too hard to capture!"

Down the back roads they chased him. As they were almost upon him, the wily robber fled into the peach trees. Try as they might, the dragoons could not find him there. Enraged, they gave up and went home in disgrace.

When they were gone, the robber stood alone in the woods and said, "O Forest, thank you for saving my worthless life once again. Can I ever repay you?"

Then, instead of saving for the poor what he had just stolen from the rich, Theo decided to bury the diamonds in the ground for his very own. He told himself that, after all, he was only an orphan and had better take care of himself first.

Then he fell into a deep sleep.
When he awoke, he was troubled, and he didn't know why.

Soon, on the evening of Valentine's Day, a figure emerged from the forest of summer in a costume of green willow branches. He hurried toward the Duke's castle, where the Sweetheart Ball was in progress.

And it wasn't two hours later, beside a frozen creek, that the robber in green dashed homeward with the dragoons at his heels. Over his shoulder was a sack filled with rubies and caramel kisses – from the Duke's own personal collection.

Again Theo fled into the forest, this time into the tangled willows of summer. Again the dragoons could find not a trace of him. Dumbfounded, they started back to their sweethearts in despair.

When they were gone, Theo stood amid the trees and said, "Forest, thank you for saving my much-improved life!" For a strange moment he thought he heard a disappointed sigh from the heart of the woods. But he told himself, "It's only your imagination."

Then he took what he had just stolen from the rich and began to bury it for himself. As he dug down to the diamonds, every-where around him – from the tip of the branches, to the trunks, to the roots – the four forests swiftly disappeared.

Theo was so busy hiding his treasure that he failed to notice. But far up the creek-bed, the dragoons chanced to look back. And what did they see but the robber alone in the moonlight, in a flat, open field, digging in the earth.

Realizing his predicament, Theo raced to and fro in the field, looking for his familiar shelter, but he was too late. The forests were gone.

The dragoons rushed down and captured him easily and recov-ered the treasure. And they took him back in chains, parading him through the countryside in an old elm-tree brown uniform they had been saving. And they threw him back in the cruel prison all over again.

Now he was given an even worse cell and even less food and even more kicks and even worse rags for a blanket than before. And the other prisoners whispered about him in more sinister voices, "It's elm-tree brown, elm-tree brown! See what happens when you become elm-tree brown!"

Weeks passed. At first all the robber could do was wish he were invisible so that he might slip out unseen from that horrible place. For now the prison was too heavily guarded to escape any other way. He wished and hoped and dreamed of being invisible, but he knew that this was impossible.

Months passed. Theo grew colder and weaker. But one thing kept him alive: the thought that somehow, someday, he would find the forests again and say he was sorry.

Three years passed.

Theo had served his time for cleverness and for escaping and for stealing the tarts, diamonds and rubies. But he still had years left to spend in jail for stealing the caramel kisses.

Then the evil Duke died and there was a new Duke. He was almost as mean as the old Duke, but he didn't give a fig about caramel kisses. So at last the robber was set free.

As they kicked Theo through the prison gate at midnight, the jailers warned that any more trouble would mean the gallows for *him!*

Though now a free man, Theo ran away fast, past the bleak orphanage, down the dangerous path, and through the tunnel in the hillside, fearful that someone must surely be chasing him.

Just when he felt too tired to continue, he came to the gallows by the crossroads. As he was gathering his strength to go on, he suddenly heard a chilling noise coming down the road. It sounded like the rattle of his chains when the dragoons had taken him back to prison, only many times worse.

Again wishing he were invisible, the robber crouched behind the gallows as two hooded figures yanked and shoved a band of small children, all chained together, past the crossroads. Orphan thieves! These evil men had kidnapped some children from the orphanage!

Forgetting his fears, Theo followed them toward the factory that snarled and buzzed in the night. As the orphans were pushed through the door, a shadow slipped in behind them.

Inside were row upon row of machines belching smoke. And everywhere were piles and foothills and mountains of shoes. And over everything – soot. Soot on the walls and soot on the ceiling and soot on the children already there chained to the shoe-stitching machines.

Theo hid behind a mountain of boots made for every size creature from giant to dwarf. He watched as the foreman shoved the new arrivals toward the machines.

Very angry, the robber grabbed first one, then the second orphan-thief from behind and clamped a giant's boot over each of their heads and knotted the laces around their necks. Then he tied smaller boots over each of their hands. Then he did the same to the foreman. And the three of them went rolling in the soot, trying to push the boots off their heads with the boots on their hands.

Then Theo leaped to a foothill of slippers and called to the children, "Fellow orphans! Follow me!" Seizing the foreman's key he freed the astonished orphans and quickly led them outside. He knew the three villains would get loose and be after them soon.

They fled through the night, hearing the escape alarm sounding.

Finally, just when the children could not go one step further, they found themselves in a flat, open field. As the moon broke through the clouds, the children looked up at Theo to help them. And he seemed to speak to the very air itself as he said, "O Forest, can you forgive me? Do what you will with me, but please help this poor band of orphans."

At that instant, with a howl, the three villains came riding from the distance on white horses with fiery eyes.

They came like the wind. And as they galloped into the field − from the tips of the branches, to the trunks, to the roots − all four of the forests reappeared.

And the small, sooty band dashed into the forest of purple-black plum trees.

The villains charged in after them on their horses. The orphans and Theo were close by, but they blended perfectly with the trees. The villains searched and they snarled, and they gave up in a fit and galloped away.

When they were gone, Theo stood in the forest with the children around him and said simply, "O Forest, we thank you."

Then he took the children through each of the forests and into the willows of summer. There they washed in a brook and ate some berries. And Theo told them how the next day they would build a house, and how the forests would be their home.

Later that night, when the children were asleep, Theo went deeper into the woods to gather soft willow branches for blankets. When he returned with the branches the children were wide awake and watching for him. They were so glad to see him they couldn't believe their eyes. They had thought this was a dream and that they would wake up back in the factory.

But he reassured them. And the children fell asleep again, a more peaceful sleep now. Theo sat against a tree trunk, resting and thinking. He thought of all those who hated the sight of elm-tree brown. He thought of the many times the forests had helped him by making him almost invisible. And he could not remember when anyone had ever been glad to see him – until tonight.

He sat against the tree and watched over the children for the rest of the night to make sure they were all safe and sound. And from that time on he watched over them in the forests till they were safely and happily grown.

And he never again wished to be invisible.